Magic Ballerina™

Holly and the Rose Garden

Darcey Bussell

HarperCollins *Children's Books*

To Phoebe and Zoe, as they are the inspiration
behind Magic Ballerina.

Contents

Prologue

*In the soft, pale light, the girl stood
with her head bent and her hands
held lightly in front of her.
There was a moment's silence and then
the first notes of the music began.
For as long as the girl could remember
music had seemed to tell her of
another world – a magical, exciting
world – that lay far, far away.
She always felt if she could just
close her eyes and lose herself,
then she would get there.
Maybe this time. As the music
swirled inside her, she swept
her arms above her head, rose on to
her toes and began to dance…*

The Rose Garden

Holly Wilde skipped down the steps of her ballet school. Twirling around, she thought about the class she had just finished. Her teacher, Madame Za-Za, had been teaching them to dance like baby swans. They were holding an open day for parents and that was the dance Holly's class were going to be performing.

Feeling happy, Holly danced a few of the steps. As she moved forward, stepping first on to one leg and then the other, a picture of her mum doing the same dance up on her pointes a few years ago came into her mind. Holly's happiness ebbed away slightly. Her parents, who were divorced, both worked for different ballet companies, which meant they were away travelling a lot. Holly had come to live with her aunt and uncle.

It had been hard at first, but it had helped that an amazing thing had happened to her. She'd been given a pair of red ballet shoes that were magic! They had the power to whisk her away to Enchantia – a land where characters from all the different ballets lived.

It was wonderful to have magic in her life, but it didn't stop Holly missing her mum and dad. Before she had come to live with her aunt and uncle, she and her mum had travelled everywhere together.

Holly sighed as she walked through the ballet-school gates. She couldn't help wishing that she was going home to show her mum the steps she was learning for the open day.

A car drew up. It was Holly's aunt.

"Hi, Holly!" she said and smiled.

"Hi," Holly replied, opening the door.

"There's a nice surprise waiting for you at home," her aunt said. "Your costume for the open day has arrived."

Holly brightened up. "Oh, wow!" She couldn't wait to get back!

As soon as they got home, Holly hurried inside. On the kitchen table was a white tutu and a white headdress made of gorgeous feathers. She picked it up and ran

upstairs. After changing into the costume, she got her red ballet shoes out of her bag and put them on. Walking over to the mirror, a sigh of delight escaped her. The costume was so beautiful! Holly touched the net of the tutu. Her arms crossed in front of her, she did an experimental *plié* and then moved with small light steps to the side.

Catching sight of herself in the mirror, she paused. *Oh, Mum*, she thought, *if you were here with me, we could dance together and practise like we used to.*

A wave of loneliness swept over her, but then Holly was distracted by a tingling in her feet. Glancing down she saw that her shoes were glowing.

The magic's working! she realised feeling a thrill of excitement. *I must be going to Enchantia again!*

She started to spin round and round, and the next second she was whirled away in a cloud of glittering colours.

Holly's feet touched down on solid ground and as the magical haze cleared, she saw that she was standing in a beautiful garden. There were roses everywhere – white ones, red ones, pink ones. Holly looked about her. Where was she? And where was her friend the White Cat? He was usually there to meet her whenever she arrived in Enchantia.

But just at that moment, Holly heard a loud shrieking cry.

"H-hello?" Holly called warily.

There was another loud shriek and out from behind a bush strode a peacock. His body was bright blue and he had golden eyes. On his head was a crest that looked almost like a little crown. His long tail of feathers trailed on the ground after him. Seeing Holly, he stared.

Holly stepped backwards uncertainly. The bird's beak looked very sharp and he had sharp claws on his feet too.

He looked her up and down intently and then his eyes seemed suddenly to glitter with approval. "Well, helllllllo there!"

His tail feathers rose and snapped open, like an enormous fan. "And who might you be, my pretty little one?"

"I'm Holly," she stammered.

The peacock stalked towards her. "Do you come here often?"

"Um…" Holly said. "Well…"

"No tail, but what fabulous feathers you have," the peacock interrupted, examining her feathery headdress. "I like them!"

"Feathers!"

Holly's hand flew to her head, as she realised that they must be confusing him into thinking she was a bird! "Oh, but they're not real. I'm a girl you see, not a—"

The peacock cawed with delight. "And I am a boy! We shall be married!"

"Married!" Holly exclaimed. "But we can't be! No!"

"No?" The peacock chuckled. "Of course we must, my sweetest swan-ling!" He lifted a claw and wagged it at her. "No one, but no one, would ever say no to Peregrine the peacock."

Pulling a golden hand mirror out from under his wing, he admired himself. "Am I not the most handsome, most sophisticated, and most perfectly perfect peacock you have ever seen in the whole of Enchantia?"

Looking at himself smugly, he blew himself a small kiss before tucking the mirror away and turning back to Holly.

"You and I are the perfect match, even if you don't have a tail. We shall live here,

strolling through the roses, pecking at the insects, sharing the juicy worms. Together forever."

He ran a claw through his crest and fixed her with an expectant look. "Well, what do you say?"

Holly backed away. "Look, I'm really very sorry, but you've got it wrong, I can't marry you. I'm not a—"

A massive roar from behind her drowned out her words. "Beauty! You're back!"

Peregrine screeched in alarm and Holly swung round. Behind her there was a huge man, with the head and shoulders of a giant beast!

The beast's monstrous face was full of hope, but as she looked at him, his

expression changed to one of anguish.

"No!" he growled despairingly. "You are not my Beauty!"

Holly stood, petrified with fear.

"Trespasser!" the beast roared. He marched down the slope and, picking her up as easily as if she was a doll, threw her over his shoulder.

Holly heard the peacock screech again. "My love! Peregrine will save you!"

He flew at the beast, but as he did so, the beast muttered a word.

For a moment, Holly thought she saw a flash of white fur behind the peacock, but then, in a swirl of light, she and the beast were whisked away…

In the Castle

Holly was dropped with a thud on to a hard floor. The beast who had whisked her away was standing before her, his lion-like face furious. She scrambled to her feet. She was in a bedroom. There were big windows with stone windowsills, a blue rug and a pretty patchwork quilt on the bed.

"How dare you trespass in my garden,

child!" the beast roared. "You will stay here until you have learned your lesson!"

Walking out, he slammed the door and turned the key in the lock.

Holly took a trembling breath. She'd had some strange adventures in Enchantia, but this seemed the strangest of the lot. First the love-struck peacock and now being locked in this room by a beast! What was going on?

She stared at the door, remembering the beast's shout in the garden when he'd first seen her. "Beauty!" he'd said. Holly's forehead furrowed. Could he be from the story of *Beauty and the Beast*? She'd watched the DVD lots when she was little and she knew there was a ballet of it too.

If he is the Beast from Beauty and the Beast

then he isn't really bad, she comforted herself by thinking.

When she looked out of the window, she could see she was in a castle. The room was in one of the towers and beneath her were roofs and turrets. From her viewpoint, she could see the gardens. Being so high up made her feel a bit wobbly, but as she started to move away from the window, she heard her name being called.

"Holly!"

She gasped. The White Cat was climbing over one of the small roofs below, looking up at her. As usual, he was wearing his golden waistcoat and had his hat on his head.

"Cat!" cried Holly, her heart leaping.

The White Cat waved anxiously. "Oh, my glittering whiskers! I am glad to have found you. Hang on. I'll be with you in two shakes of a mouse's tail – I hope!" His voice shook nervously.

"Be careful!" Holly cried. She knew he

didn't like heights any more than she did.

Holly watched with her heart in her mouth, as her friend jumped on to a small ledge and started to climb rapidly up the tower. Reaching the window ledge, he scrambled over and landed in a heap on the floor.

"Phew!" he said, taking a deep, shaky breath. Holly rushed to help him up. But the White Cat was already leaping to his feet.

Now he was inside, his fear seemed to have vanished. He spun round and jumped into the air, his arms above his head, his legs thrown back. On landing, he held out his front paw to Holly.

She took it in delight and, giggling, they

curtsied and bowed to
each other before
hugging.

"Are you OK?"
Holly asked. "It
must have been
really scary to
climb up all that
way."

"It was, but I had
to do it. I couldn't leave
you up here alone," said the cat.
"Oh, my shimmering tail, are you all right,
Holly? You must have been terrified when
the Beast grabbed you like that. I arrived in
the rose garden just as he whisked you
away."

"It was scary," Holly admitted. "Is he the Beast from *Beauty and the Beast*?"

"The very same," the White Cat told her. "Poor creature. He's having a hard time. Please forgive him for scaring you. Come and sit down and I'll tell you what's been going on."

They sat down on the bed together. "So, you know the story of *Beauty and the Beast*?" the cat asked.

Holly nodded. "Beauty's father is travelling home from market and he stops and picks a rose from a garden, because Beauty's asked for one, and the Beast, who is really an enchanted prince, sees him and gets angry. He only lets Beauty's father go because he promises that he will send his

youngest daughter to stay with the Beast."

"Exactly so!" declared the White Cat. "Beauty comes to the castle and the Beast falls in love with her. She seems to have fallen in love with him too, so we thought it would only be a matter of time before the enchantment on the Prince would be broken. They were getting on brilliantly—"

"But then Beauty's father gets ill and she gets called to go back home!" Holly interrupted, remembering the story.

"Yes, that's exactly where we're at," said the White Cat. "Beauty hasn't returned to the Beast like she said she would and he is really unhappy. He's decided that she doesn't love him after all. That's why he's in such a miserable mood."

31

"Can't someone just go to her father's and tell Beauty how much the Beast is missing her?" Holly suggested.

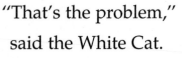

"That's the problem," said the White Cat. "Beauty never got to her father's! When she left the castle, she just disappeared. I've been trying to use my magic to see where she is now, but it isn't working." He looked anxious. "If I can't use my magic to see her, it must mean she's been captured by someone using strong powers to stop us

from finding her. Wherever she is, we have to find her and bring her back. The longer the Beast is away from Beauty, the more his heart breaks. He could even die."

"What can I do to help?" said Holly quickly. "Maybe I could try to find Beauty?"

The cat shook his head. "The King has sent people out all over the land to do that. What would be a help, is if you could keep the Beast busy until Beauty comes back. Talk to him, amuse him, take his mind off her if you can."

Holly wasn't sure she liked the thought of looking after the Beast, but if that's what the White Cat needed her to do, then so be it. "Of course," she said.

"Thank you!" The White Cat hugged her.

"Just don't tell the Beast that Beauty has been taken away by someone wicked. He thinks she's still at her father's. We're all worried that if the Beast learns that someone has captured Beauty, he might get so cross, he'll go on the rampage and hurt himself – or others."

The White Cat went to the window. "I'll climb down and explain to the Beast who you are, then I'm sure he'll let you out." He took a deep breath. "OK, here I go. See you soon!"

"Bye!" Holly stared for a moment at the space where he had been. Worry flickered through her at the thought of looking after the Beast. *Oh, goodness*, she thought. *What have I let myself in for?*

A Crazy Castle

It could only have been a matter of ten minutes later, when Holly heard a key turning in the door and the Beast and the White Cat came in. Holly swallowed. Even though she now knew the Beast was friendly, he still looked pretty scary.

His voice rumbled out. "I am sorry, Holly."

She could see the unhappiness in his dark eyes.

"I should not have locked you in here. The White Cat has told me who you are."

"It's OK." Holly felt almost shy for once, which was quite unlike her. "You… you must be missing Beauty a lot."

The Beast nodded heavily.

"I'm sure she'll be back soon," said Holly, trying to be as bright as she could. "And while you're waiting, I can keep you company."

"I must be off," said the White Cat, giving Holly a meaningful look. "I have business to attend to. But before I go, the servants are preparing lunch for us. Shall we go down?"

"Oh, yes!" Holly said eagerly.

She followed the White Cat and the Beast out of the bedroom and down the wide sweeping staircase. To her astonishment, she saw plates of cold meats and bowls of fruit moving through the air, as if by magic.

Holly stared as a basket of bread whisked by. "The food is flying about!"

The White Cat saw her face. "Oh, sorry, Holly, I should've explained. When the Beast was enchanted all his servants turned invisible."

Looking round in wonder, Holly followed the White Cat towards the dining room, where a delicious feast had been laid out on the table. Chairs moved as they approached and were pushed in by invisible hands as they sat down. The fruit punch poured itself into her glass and food started moving down the table towards her.

"You'll get used to it in the end," the White Cat grinned, starting to tuck in.

The Beast didn't seem to want to eat

anything. He just paced up and down by
the fireplace.

"Music!" the White Cat cried.

A selection of instruments jumped into
the air and began to play a lively polka. All
around Holly, objects suddenly lifted up –
brooms and mops, chairs and small tables.

They all twirled around the room, held by the invisible servants, who were using them as partners so the Beast could watch the dancing. It was the strangest thing Holly had ever seen – but she loved it! Her feet started to tap.

"Come on!" said the White Cat. Grabbing her hands, he pulled her into the dance. Holly glanced over at the Beast. Even he was smiling slightly now.

At last, Holly and the White Cat collapsed at the table again. They had ice cream for dessert and then it was time for her friend to leave.

"Bye, Cat," said Holly, hugging him on

the steps of the castle.

"Take care of the Beast," he whispered into her ears.

"I will," she promised.

The White Cat swept into an elegant bow. "Goodbye, Your Highness," he said to the Beast. "Beauty will be back soon. I have no doubt about it."

He twirled his tail about him in a circle, silver sparks shot into the air and suddenly he was gone.

Holly looked at the empty air. She hoped he'd come back soon, but now she had a job to do too. Fixing a smile on her face, she

41

turned to the Beast. "Will you show me round the castle, please? And then, maybe we could read or talk or play games?"

"As you wish," the Beast said and, with a sigh, he turned and led the way inside.

° ☉ ∴* ☆ ☉ ∴*. ☆ ☉ ∴*. ☆ ☉ ∴*. °

The Beast took Holly all round the castle until they finished up in one of the big lounges. Holly found a library of books and tried reading to the Beast, but he simply stared into space and hardly seemed to be listening.

"Why hasn't she come back?" he sighed. "She said she would only be gone for a day."

"Would you like me to dance for you?"

Holly suggested, remembering how the Beast had seemed to enjoy the dancing at lunchtime. He nodded.

Holly went to find some of the musical instruments still being held by the servants. Soon they were playing the lively music for the dance of the baby swans that Holly was learning at ballet school. Holly danced across the floor. It was easier without having to try and be perfectly in time with the other girls. She kept her movements as light and as fast as possible, trying to feel like she really was a bird.

Pas de chats, pas de chats. She leaped sideways again and again, and then pointed her feet quickly in front of her, one after the other, over and over. Dancing

forward, finally, she stopped in an *arabesque* and finished by kneeling down, perfectly in time with the music.

The Beast clapped. "Very good!" he rumbled. "That was lovely." And, for a

moment, he looked almost happy.

Holly smiled, her cheeks flushed. She went to fetch a glass of water from the side of the room. As she did so, she saw a movement at the large windows that looked out on to the garden. She gasped. It was the peacock she'd met earlier! She'd almost forgotten about him. But now he was tapping on the glass to attract her attention. Holly waved her hand at him. "Go away!" she mouthed.

The peacock seemed to think she was greeting him and waved his fan of feathers, before blowing her a kiss. Now he'd seen her dance like a bird, he looked more love-struck than ever!

Holly turned her back on him. "Shall I

dance for you some more?" she asked the Beast.

But he had turned away. "Maybe later," he said grouchily, back to his old self. "I'm going to rest now until supper."

Still, he did give a slight smile. "My heart feels easier after watching you dance. Thank you, Holly."

Holly breathed a sigh of relief as he left the room. She was glad she had made a little difference to him, but how long could she go on like this? She couldn't dance all day!

Behind her, she heard a screech and saw the peacock dancing from one leg to the other. She groaned under her breath. If it wasn't enough that she had to keep the

Beast amused, she also seemed to have
attracted the attentions of a mad peacock!

Oh, White Cat, she thought. *I hope you
come back soon!*

The Magic Mirror

All that evening, Holly entertained the
Beast. She danced and talked and read. It
was exhausting, and she was very glad
when he decided to go to bed and she was
able to turn in for the night too. She
snuggled down under the patchwork quilt.
Outside, she was sure she heard the
peacock screech. He'd been walking round

the castle gardens all day and whenever she came to a window, he'd dashed forward eagerly. *I'd better talk to him in the morning,* Holly decided. *I really do need to convince him that I'm not actually a bird!*

°⊙˙*˙☆˙⊙˙*˙☆˙⊙˙*˙☆˙⊙˙*˙°

The next day, the Beast's mood didn't seem to have improved. As he sat down despondently at the breakfast table, he sighed and pushed his bacon and eggs around his plate, not trying even a mouthful. "I dreamed that Beauty was here this morning," he said mournfully. "But she still hasn't come back."

"She's probably just staying with her father a little longer," said Holly as she crossed her fingers under the table.

The Beast's head drooped. "Or maybe she's just forgotten me. Oh, if only I had the magic mirror. The person holding it can see whoever they love, wherever they are in it, but Beauty took it with her."

Holly felt very glad the Beast didn't have this magic mirror or he would soon realise that Beauty wasn't at her father's after all!

Quickly, she changed the subject. "Will you take me out into the garden after breakfast?" she asked the Beast. "I'd love to see around the grounds."

The Beast nodded. "Very well."

When Holly had finished breakfast, they walked out into the sunny gardens. Almost immediately there was a loud screech of delight and the peacock stepped out from behind a bush. "Good morrow, my sweetest songbird!" he exclaimed. "You look truly divine this morning – as beautiful as a juicy brown worm peeping out of the grass, as delicious as an insect buzzing through the—"

The Beast's growl cut him off. "Be quiet, peacock, and go away!"

"Such coarseness!" The peacock looked haughty. He turned his back on the Beast. "Tarry here no longer, my sugar swan," he said to Holly. "Flutter your feathers. Let us fly away together. What do you say?"

"Go away," the Beast repeated through gritted teeth.

The peacock opened his mouth.

"NOW!" the Beast roared in an enormous voice.

Even the peacock didn't dare to disobey this time. He flew off in a huff. Holly's heart sank. She'd have to explain to him later. But now she had to help the Beast, who was looking very sad.

"My sweet-natured Beauty likes everyone she comes across, even that irritating bird," he said.

"You've got some beautiful roses in the garden," Holly said, trying to distract him. She ran forward to a bush that had flowers the colour of a pink satin ballet shoe. "This

one is lovely."

"I know. I used to place one of those roses outside Beauty's bedroom door every morning." The Beast clutched his chest and shut his eyes. "Oh, it hurts, Holly."

"Your heart?" she said anxiously.

He nodded.

"Look, sit down." Holly guided him over to a bench. "It'll be OK."

Hesitantly, she touched his shaggy mane. The Beast closed his eyes. Holly stroked

Magic Ballerina

his fur and gradually, he began to go to sleep. When his breathing deepened and he started to snore slightly, she buried her head in her hands. How was she going to keep him occupied all day?

"Holly!" She heard a whisper and looked up with a start. The White Cat was peeping out from behind a red rosebush. "Over here!" he hissed.

Holly ran as fast as she could to him.

"Have you found Beauty?" she asked.

The White Cat shook his head despondently. "No. Oh, if only we had the Beast's magic mirror."

"But isn't it good we haven't got the mirror?" said Holly. "Otherwise, the Beast would look in it, but not be able to see

Beauty, and then he'd realise she was being kept somewhere by magic."

The cat shook his head. "No, it wouldn't work like that. The mirror would always show him where Beauty is because it links them through love."

"Ah, love! Sweet love," cried Peregrine the peacock, suddenly returning and overhearing the conversation. He looked adoringly at Holly, who tried to ignore him.

"What do you mean?" she asked the White Cat.

"Love is more powerful than even the strongest magic," the cat replied. "It reaches across the miles, no matter how far apart two people are or what barriers are in the way. But we're wasting our time discussing this. It is of no use to us, because Beauty took the mirror with her."

At that point, Peregrine strode forward. "If you need a mirror, you can borrow mine, my sweet."

"Thank you, but what we need is a magic

mirror," said Holly. "It's—"

"It's that one!" the White Cat exclaimed, as the peacock pulled his mirror out from under his wing. "I'd know it anywhere. Oh, my glittering whiskers!"

He jumped to his feet. "The peacock's got the magic mirror!"

Finding Beauty

The peacock squawked in surprise.

"That's really the magic mirror?" said Holly, gazing at the looking glass in the peacock's claw.

The White Cat nodded. "Where did you get it from?" he asked the peacock.

"I found it on the ground, just outside the garden gate last week," Peregrine

replied, looking as surprised as them. "I thought someone must have thrown it away."

"Outside the gate. Oh, my gleaming eyes! Beauty must have dropped it when she was captured," the White Cat breathed.

"Then we can use it to find out where she is!" cried Holly. "Oh, Peregrine, please can we borrow it for a few minutes?"

The peacock held the mirror out. "Of course, my little sugar swan."

"Thank you!" Holly cried. "So, what do we do with it?" she asked the cat. "If it's a mirror of love, doesn't the Beast have to look in it, to see where Beauty is?"

"He just needs to be touching it," the White Cat said. "Then, it will show the person he loves best."

"Stuff and nonsense!" said Peregrine. "When I am holding that mirror it always shows me myself!"

"Exactly," the White Cat muttered under his breath.

Holly hid a grin and turned her thoughts to the matter in hand. "I'll take the mirror and put it next to the Beast. Only, I hope he doesn't wake up!"

She ran over to the bench and sat down as quietly as she could. The Beast was still snoring. Carefully, she brought the mirror round to his side. As she did so, she caught a glimpse of a dark-haired woman in it. The woman was smiling with a group of other ballerinas, as they warmed up in a ballet studio. For a moment, Holly couldn't do anything but stare. It was her mum!

"Holly!" the White Cat hissed from the bushes. "Hurry up!"

Holly hastily put the mirror down and forced the image to the back of her mind. Now wasn't the time. She pushed the mirror closer, until it was just touching the Beast's leg. Then, making sure she wasn't touching it herself, she peered at the glass.

What was she going to see?

A mist travelled swiftly across the mirror's surface. As it cleared, Holly saw a beautiful girl sitting on a bench in a small wooden summerhouse. She had her hands wrapped around her knees and she was

crying. In the corner of the mirror, Holly could see something white and feathery, but she couldn't quite make out what it was. Visible through the window of the summerhouse was a castle made of pale grey stone. A black flag was flying from the top turret with a picture of a silver serpent on it.

Taking the mirror, Holly raced back across the lawn to where the White Cat and the peacock were waiting. "I saw Beauty!" Holly described the wooden summerhouse and the flag on the castle, and the White Cat caught his breath.

"Then that means Beauty is in the grounds of the Dark Witch. She's the one who enchanted the Prince in the first place.

She must have realised that Beauty and the Beast had fallen in love and that her spell was about to be broken, so she's captured Beauty." He shook his head. "I thought it might be her, so I checked her castle out earlier with my magic, but there was no sign of Beauty anywhere inside. I guess the Dark Witch must have known we would search the castle, so she decided to imprison Beauty in the summerhouse to trick us!"

"At least we know where Beauty is now," said Holly. "Will your magic take us there?"

The White Cat nodded.

"I shall come too!" cried the peacock. "I'm not letting you go into danger on your own, my love." He ruffled his tail feathers

proudly. "Peregrine shall be by your side."

"You can't come," protested Holly. It was going to be hard enough to try and rescue Beauty, without the peacock swishing his great tail and screeching everywhere!

The peacock stepped between Holly and the White Cat. "You will not go without me."

"Oh, let him come," said the cat. "There's no time to waste." He drew a circle with his long tail and, grabbing Holly's hands, he pulled her inside. Peregrine jumped in too. "Here we go!" the White Cat cried, as the magic spun all three of them away.

They were set down behind a large stone
statue of a snake, in the gardens of the grey
castle.

"It's just like in the mirror!" whispered
Holly, as she saw the tall grey building and
a little way off in the distance, the small

wooden summerhouse. She peeped around the statue. "I can't see any guards. Why don't we just go and unlock the door or break a window or something?"

"Oh, my brave, beautiful love," sighed the peacock. "Such courage. Such cleverness!"

"Ssh!" Holly said hastily, seeing he was about to screech in delight. "We've got to be quiet. Please! Here." She handed him the mirror. The peacock held it in his claw, and looking into it, he waggled his crest happily at himself.

With the peacock suitably distracted, Holly turned back to the White Cat. "I'll go on to the summerhouse."

"You're not going on your own," he said.

"We'll go together. Ready?" Holly nodded and they ran across the grass.

As they neared the summerhouse, Holly felt a tingle run through her and saw several sparks fly from the White Cat's whiskers, just like they usually did when he sensed magic. She didn't have time to think about it, though. They had to rescue Beauty!

On reaching the summerhouse, they found big metal bolts across the doorway, but luckily no lock. The White Cat pulled them back and threw open the door. Beauty was inside! She gave a startled cry and jumped to her feet. "White Cat and… and…"

"I'm Holly," said Holly quickly.

Beauty looked at Holly's feet. "The girl

with the red shoes! Oh, you've come to rescue us!"

"Us?" Holly echoed, wondering what she meant, but the White Cat was already speaking. "There's no time to waste, Beauty. We must get you back to the Beast. His heart is breaking."

"I know, I can feel it here," said Beauty, touching her own heart. "And there's my father too. He's ill."

"It's all right. Your father is very worried about you, but he has recovered from his illness," the White Cat said. "The Beast, however, does need you."

Holly grabbed Beauty's hands. "The White Cat will use his magic to take us back to him straight away."

A harsh voice snapped through the air. "Oh, will he now?"

They all swung round to see a scary old woman standing behind them. She had jet-black eyes and a wand in her hand. Holly felt her stomach turn to ice. It had to be the Dark Witch!

True Love

Holly, the White Cat and Beauty froze as the Dark Witch cackled. "You lot are going nowhere!"

"How… how did you know we were here?" stammered the White Cat.

"Did you honestly think I would be so stupid as to leave this girl unguarded? Fool! I had a magic barrier in place. As soon as you crossed it, I knew there was trouble afoot."

Holly remembered the tingle that had run through her and the sparks she had seen flying off the White Cat's whiskers. They should have realised.

The Dark Witch threw back her head. "No one is going to free Beauty. She and the bird are staying here!"

The bird? Holly wondered what she meant.

"They will stay and so will you!" The Dark Witch raised her wand and pointed it at the White Cat and Holly. But just then, there was a loud screech and Peregrine flew out from behind the statue. "No!" he screamed. "You shall not harm my love!"

The Dark Witch turned round in surprise.

"Get off me, bird!" she cried, staggering backwards as Peregrine flew at her with his beak open.

"Never!" he cried valiantly. "Peregrine shall fight to the death to save his love!" Bringing his legs up, he kicked out with his feet. At the back of his legs were two sharp spurs, like extra-long claws. They caught in the sleeves of the Dark Witch's dress and pinned her to the wooden wall of the summerhouse. She tried to wave her wand, but her arm was caught fast!

"Go!" Peregrine cried bravely to the others as the witch shrieked and screamed and kicked. "Leave this place! I will hold her here."

The White Cat leaped on to the grass and

drew a circle with his tail. Holly grabbed Beauty's hand and pulled her forward into it.

"Pandora!" Beauty cried, looking back at the summerhouse. "Come with us! You must!"

There was a squawk and out of the summerhouse flew a large white bird. The sparkles were whirling around the circle, which meant that the magic was about to work. "Peregrine!" she shouted. "You can't stay here! You must come too!"

"Whatever you say, my love!" Peregrine released the witch and flew into the circle with one flap of his wings.

"NO!" the Dark Witch shouted, thrusting out her wand. There was a green flash, but

she was too late. The White Cat's magic swirled around and spun them away…

They all landed in a heap in the grass back in the Beast's garden. For a moment, Holly just lay there, blinking and trying to get her thoughts together. She felt dazed. It had all happened so fast, but at least they'd escaped. They'd got away from the Dark Witch! And now they just had to return Beauty to the Beast.

Holly scrambled to her feet and looked about at her friends. The White Cat was leaning back, rubbing his head. And Peregrine was staring open-mouthed at a beautiful snow-white peahen!

"Well, hellllllllo, gorgeous!" he said, waggling his eyebrows.The peahen cooed and looked down coyly.

"Valentino!" Beauty was running towards the bench where the Beast was still asleep. "Valentino, I'm back!"

The Beast woke with a start and stared as if he couldn't believe his eyes. "Beauty? Is that really you?"

"Yes!" She flung herself into his arms.

The Beast made a noise halfway between a growl and a cry. "You're back! My heart was breaking."

"I know!" Beauty clasped her chest. "I could feel it here. I could feel it because I love you – I love you so much!"

There was a silver flash of magic. Holly gasped and the White Cat cried out as suddenly the Beast was no longer a beast,

but a man! He was tall and very
good-looking with blond hair. He swept
Beauty into his arms. "And I love you too!"

"Oh, wow!" Holly said faintly, slowly getting to her feet.

The White Cat put his arm round her shoulders. "We did it," he said in relief. "We got Beauty back – and broke the enchantment."

"We didn't do that bit," said Holly, looking at the Prince and Beauty who were sharing a kiss. She smiled. "They did that themselves."

"And it looks as if they aren't the only ones who have found love," commented the White Cat, grinning at Holly. "I think your place in Peregrine's heart has been taken."

Holly looked round to see Peregrine and the white peahen, Pandora, staring at each other adoringly. Peregrine's tail fanned out

and he rustled his feathers. Pandora
clucked and looked very impressed.

"Who is she?" Holly asked. "And what
was she doing in the summerhouse?"

Beauty overheard. She came over, hand in
hand with the Prince. "Pandora landed in
the Dark Witch's garden while I was trapped

there. The Dark Witch caught her and locked
her up with me. She had been planning to
parade her at the celebration feast she was
going to have when Valentino's heart was
finally broken." Beauty squeezed the
Prince's hand. "Luckily, that didn't happen."

"Thanks to you both," the Prince said to
Holly and the White Cat. "I will always be
indebted to you for bringing back my
Beauty and saving me."

Holly smiled. "I'm glad we could help."

"My beautiful love," Peregrine cawed to
Pandora. "Let me give you a gift. The most
precious thing I own. I used to look in my
mirror to gaze on my own face, but now I
have you to gaze on and I have no need of it
any more."

He held the mirror out. Holly caught sight of the reflection and saw the image of Pandora in there. She smiled. Maybe Peregrine really had found true love at last!

"Thank you, my love," Pandora clucked. As she took the mirror in her own claw, an image of Peregrine formed in it. Holly and the White Cat exchanged happy looks.

The Prince turned to Beauty. "Through all my days as a lumbering beast, I wanted so much to dance with you properly. Let us dance now!" He strode to the castle. "Music!" he called.

The servants, who were no longer invisible, all came streaming out, young and old, laughing and chattering. In no time at all, the musicians were playing a beautiful waltz.

Holly watched as the Prince gathered Beauty in his arms and they danced around the garden, their eyes never leaving each other. They separated and Beauty stood on one leg, in a perfect *arabesque*, while the Prince leaped into the air, crossing his feet over before taking hold of Beauty's hand and spinning her away.

"Join in, everyone!" Beauty cried, laughing in delight.

The servants swung each other about. The White Cat grabbed Holly and began to waltz her around the rose garden. "Oh, my glimmering whiskers! It's been a great adventure!" he exclaimed.

Holly nodded happily. "It really has!"

They danced until they could dance no

more and then collapsed on a bench.
Nearby, Peregrine and Pandora were taking
it in turns to admire each other in the
mirror. Beauty and the Prince were walking
hand in hand, chatting softly.

Holly felt her feet start to tingle. "It's
time for me to go!" she cried. "Goodbye,
Cat! Goodbye, Beauty and Prince Valentino!
Bye, Pandora and Peregrine. Bye,
everyone!"

And before she knew it, the magic had
whirled around her and swept her away.

Home Again

Holly came to rest in her bedroom. As the cloud of colours cleared, she took a deep breath, her head still spinning from the magic. No time ever passed in the human world while she was away, so she knew her aunt wouldn't have missed her. *What an adventure!* she thought. In her mind, she could see Beauty and the Prince waltzing round. They had looked so perfect together – so completely in love. She was really glad that she had been able to help them.

Her eyes fell on her own mirror and she walked over to it slowly. She touched the shining surface, remembering the magic mirror in Enchantia. "I wish you were magic too, and I could see Mum," she whispered.

But as she spoke, the White Cat's words from earlier echoed in her head: Love is more powerful than even the strongest magic. It reaches across the miles, no matter how far apart you are or what barriers are in the way.

It's true, Holly realised, suddenly. *Mum might be a long way away, but I don't need to see her to know that we love each other. I'm not alone. She's always with me in some way.*

Lifting her arms, she spun on the spot gracefully, thinking about Beauty dancing with Prince Valentino. One day, just like Beauty and her Prince, she and her mum would be dancing together again. She smiled and with a light heart, pirouetted away round the room.

Darcey's Magical Masterclass

Grand Plié in 3rd position

Pretend you are bobbing down to pick a rose from the garden with this pretty move.

2.
Bend your knees outwards and crouch down, keeping your back straight and your head up. Keep your right arm in second position.

1.
Hold on to the barre with your right hand, and stand with your feet in third position, one foot placed against the instep of the other. Place your left arm out to the side in the second position.

3.
While you crouch down, your heels will come off the ground. Open your right arm further as if picking a flower on your right side. Follow this arm movement with your eyes so your head turns towards the flower.

4.
Gently stand back up, using the barre to help you. Then lower both arms to your sides and check your feet are still in third position.

Magic Ballerina
Holly and the Ice Palace

King Rat has captured the Winter Fairy
and transformed his castle into an ice palace.
Can Holly and the White Cat save her
before it's too late?

**Read on for a sneak preview
of Holly's next adventure…**

"This is as close as I dare to get," said the White Cat.

Holly didn't answer. She was too busy staring in awe at the magnificent ice palace in front of them. Its turrets and towers glowed and gleamed in silver brilliance, and, through the tall ice-spiked gates, she could see a winter garden full of ice sculptures.

"They're not real sculptures," the White Cat whispered, following Holly's gaze. "They're people that King Rat has turned into statues with his evil magic."

Holly gasped. Anger flared up inside her that this nasty rat could be so cruel, but she was puzzled, too. "What were these people doing here in the first place?" she asked.

"They each came to try and rescue the powers of the Winter Fairy," said the White Cat. "Everyone is so alarmed about how Enchantia is heating up that they're desperate to restore the natural balance of the seasons. But see what's become of them!"

"No, look, they're not all ice statues!" said Holly, suddenly spotting a young man who had appeared from round the side of the garden. He was looking furtively this way and that, as he dodged behind one ice statue after another.

"He'll be searching for the Winter Fairy," said the White Cat, in a low voice. "Just like the others."

"Oh dear, I hope he manages to keep himself hidden, so he doesn't get turned into a…"

But Holly never had a chance to finish her sentence. Instead, she gasped because the man was halfway between two statues when the front door of the palace was suddenly flung open, and there stood King Rat himself. His beady red eyes stared out from beneath grey bushy eyebrows. Whiskers sprouted from all over his face. And on his head perched a tall golden crown, which Holly thought looked ridiculous.

Spotting the intruder, his face turned purple with anger and he began yelling a chant as he swiped his sword through the air.

"Once I swish again and twice.
Now turn this mad fool into ice!"

In a flash, the man became a statue…

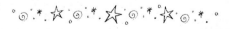

Magic Ballerina

Read all of Holly's adventures!

Magic Ballerina ™

Meet Delphie and Rosa too!

Magic Ballerina

Darcey Bussell

Buy more great Magic Ballerina books direct from HarperCollins
at 10% off recommended retail price.
FREE postage and packing in the UK.

Holly and the Dancing Cat	ISBN 978 0 00 732319 7
Holly and the Silver Unicorn	ISBN 978 0 00 732320 3
Holly and the Magic Tiara	ISBN 978 0 00 732321 0
Holly and the Rose Garden	ISBN 978 0 00 732322 7
Holly and the Ice Palace	ISBN 978 0 00 732323 4
Holly and the Land of Sweets	ISBN 978 0 00 732324 1

All priced at £4.99

To purchase by Visa/Mastercard/Switch simply call
08707871724 or fax on **08707871725**

To pay by cheque, send a copy of this form with a cheque made payable to
'HarperCollins Publishers' to: Mail Order Dept. (Ref: BOB4),
HarperCollins Publishers, Westerhill Road, Bishopbriggs, G64 2QT,
making sure to include your full name, postal address and phone number.

From time to time HarperCollins may wish to use your personal data
to send you details of other HarperCollins publications and offers.
If you wish to receive information on other HarperCollins publications
and offers please tick this box ☐

Do not send cash or currency. Prices correct at time of press.
Prices and availability are subject to change without notice.
Delivery overseas and to Ireland incurs a £2 per book postage and packing charge.